This Walker book
belongs to:

_____

First published 2009 by Walker Books Ltd
87 Vauxhall Walk, London SE11 5HJ

This edition published 2012

2 4 6 8 10 9 7 5 3 1

This book has been typeset in Gill Sans MT Schoolbook

Printed in China

British Library Cataloguing in Publication Data:
a catalogue record for this book is available
from the British Library

ISBN 978-1-4063-4045-7

www.walker.co.uk

Tilly and
her friends
all live
together in
a little yellow
house...

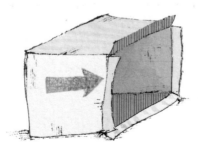

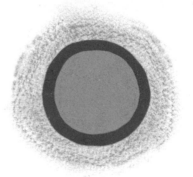

Where's
Tumpty?

Polly Dunbar

WALKER BOOKS
AND SUBSIDIARIES
LONDON • BOSTON • SYDNEY • AUCKLAND

Tumpty
had his eyes
closed.

Tightly closed.

"Hello, Tumpty,"
said Tilly.
"What are you
doing?"

"I'm hiding," Tumpty said.

"You can't see me."

But Tilly **could** see Tumpty.

So Tumpty tried hiding
under a large cardboard box,
with his eyes tightly closed.

"What is
Tumpty doing?"
asked
Hector.

"He's
hiding!"
said Tilly.

"But I can see him," laughed Hector.

So Tumpty tried hiding behind a pot plant,
under a large cardboard box,
with his eyes tightly closed.

"What is   "He's
Tumpty   hiding,"
up to?"   said
asked Pru.   Hector.

"Don't be daft," said Pru. "I can see him."

So Tumpty tried hiding upside down, behind
a pot plant, under a large cardboard box,
with his eyes tightly closed.

"Ha ha ha!"
laughed Doodle.
"Look at Tumpty."

"He's hiding," laughed Pru.

"Humpf," said Tumpty.

"Tumpty is so **funny,"** said Tiptoe.

Everybody laughed and laughed.

They laughed and laughed

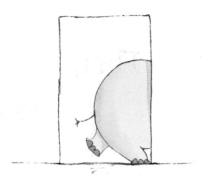

and  laughed.

"Hang on,"
said Doodle.
"Where's
Tumpty?"

"He must
be hiding,"
Hector
said.

"Let's look
for him,"
said
Tilly.

"Are you in here?"
said Tilly,
looking in
the cupboard.

Tumpty wasn't there.

"I bet he's behind the curtains!" said Hector.

Tumpty wasn't there.

"Nope,
he's not here either,"
said Doodle,
looking under the table.

"Perhaps
he's in
the biscuit tin,"
said
Tiptoe.

Tumpty definitely wasn't
there, but there were
some **biscuits.**

"I miss Tumpty," said Doodle.

"Perhaps he's really gone," said Tiptoe.

"For ever!" cried Hector.

"I'm here!" trumpeted Tumpty,
jumping out from behind the sofa.
"I was only hiding!"

"Hurrah! We love

you, Tumpty!" said everyone.

"You're so clever at hiding," said Tilly.

"I know," said Tumpty,

and he finished off all the biscuits.

The End

Polly Dunbar

Polly Dunbar is one of today's most exciting young author-illustrators, her warm and witty books captivating children the world over.

Polly based the Tilly and Friends stories on her own experience of sharing a house with friends. Tilly, Hector, Tumpty, Doodle, Tiptoe and Pru are all very different and they don't always get on. But in the little yellow house, full of love and laughter, no one can be sad or cross for long!

ISBN 978-1-4063-4024-2

ISBN 978-1-4063-4048-8

ISBN 978-1-4063-4049-5

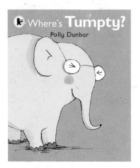

ISBN 978-1-4063-4045-7

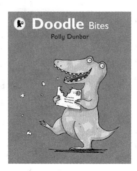

ISBN 978-1-4063-4046-4

ISBN 978-1-4063-4047-1

"Nobody can draw anything more instantly loveable than one of Dunbar's characters."
Independent on Sunday

Available from all good booksellers

www.walker.co.uk